Dear Parent:
Your child's love of reading starts here!

Every child learns to read in a different way and at his or her own speed. You can help your young reader improve and become more confident by encouraging his or her own interests and abilities. You can also guide your child's spiritual development by reading stories with biblical values and Bible stories, like I Can Read! books published by Zonderkidz. From books your child reads with you to the first books he or she reads alone, there are I Can Read! books for every stage of reading:

SHARED READING
Basic language, word repetition, and whimsical illustrations, ideal for sharing with your emergent reader.

BEGINNING READING
Short sentences, familiar words, and simple concepts for children eager to read on their own.

READING WITH HELP
Engaging stories, longer sentences, and language play for developing readers.

READING ALONE
Complex plots, challenging vocabulary, and high-interest topics for the independent reader.

ADVANCED READING
Short paragraphs, chapters, and exciting themes for the perfect bridge to chapter books.

I Can Read! books have introduced children to the joy of reading since 1957. Featuring award-winning authors and illustrators and a fabulous cast of beloved characters, I Can Read! books set the standard for beginning readers.

A lifetime of discovery begins with the magical words **"I Can Read!"**

Visit www.icanread.com for information on enriching your child's reading experience.
Visit www.zonderkidz.com for more Zonderkidz I Can Read! titles.

"Be kind and compassionate
to one another."
—*Ephesians 4:32*

ZONDERKIDZ

Princess Sisters Treasury
Copyright © 2012 by Zonderkidz

Requests for information should be addressed to:

Zonderkidz, 5300 *Patterson Ave. SE, Grand Rapids, Michigan 49530*

Library of Congress Cataloging-in-Publication Data
Young, Jeanna Stolle, 1968 –
    Princess sisters treasury / written by Jeanna Young & Jacqueline Johnson ;
illustrated by Omar Aranda.
        v. cm. – (I can read) (Princess parables)
    ISBN 978-0-310-73251-8
    [1. Princesses–Fiction 2. Christian life–Fiction. 3. Charity–Fiction. 4. Parables.] I. Johnson,
Jacqueline Kinney, 1943- II. Aranda, Omar, ill. III. Title.
    PZ7.Y8654Prs 2013
    [E]–dc23
                                                   2012029842

Princess Grace and Poppy ISBN 9780310726777 (2012)
Princess Faith's Garden Surprise ISBN 9780310732495 (2012)
Princess Charity's Golden Heart ISBN 9780310732488 (2012)

Editor: Mary Hassinger
Design: Diane Mielke

Printed in China

13 14 15 16 17 /DSC/ 7 6 5 4 3 2

ZONDERkidz

I Can Read!™

BEGINNING
1
READING

The Princess Parables™

Princess Grace
and Poppy

Story inspired by **Jeanna Young & Jacqueline Johnson**
Pictures by **Omar Aranda**

RANCHO CUCAMONGA PUBLIC LIBRARY KIDSMOBILE

Princess Grace lives in a castle.

She has four sisters.

They are Joy, Faith, Charity, and Hope.

Their daddy is the king!

4

5

One day, Grace dropped a vase.

While she was picking up

flowers, Grace heard a noise.

"Meow, meow, meow!"

Grace looked in the closet

under the stairs.

She said, "Five kittens!

How did you get in here?"

Joy, Faith, Charity,

and Hope went to see too.

Hope said, "It is five kittens!"

The king looked at the princesses.

The king looked at the kittens.

Grace said, "Daddy, I found

five kittens.

May we keep them, please?"

The king said, "We will talk about it."

Faith prayed, "Dear God, thank you for the kittens.

If daddy says yes, I promise to take care of them."

The king let the kittens
stay in the castle.

The princesses helped Grace with
one kitten each.

Princess Grace named her special
kitten Poppy.

Poppy was a happy kitten.

She loved to run and play.

Poppy even played at the

dinner table.

The princesses laughed.

But the king said,

"Grace, please stop Poppy."

Grace said, "Poppy! Please come

here."

Every day the princesses played
with the kittens.

Princess Charity said,

"My kitten has a green bow."

Princess Faith said,

"My kitten has a blue dress."

But Poppy was Grace's favorite
kitten of the litter.
She loved to play.
Poppy played hide-and-seek.
Grace called, "Where are you,
Poppy?"

Poppy ran from Grace.

She ran so fast! Boom!

Silly Poppy ran into the king's feet.

The king smiled.

"You are a special kitten, Poppy."

Then, one day, Princess Grace
could not find Poppy.

"One … two … three … four …
Poppy? Where are you?" Grace
cried out.

Her little kitten was not with
the others.

Where could she be?

The king found Grace in the garden.

The princess was praying.

"Dear God, please take care

of little Poppy.

Keep her safe.

I love her very much."

The king said, "God hears

your prayers, Grace.

Ask him to keep Poppy safe.

And I will help you look for her."

Joy, Faith, Charity, Hope, and Grace looked all over the castle. Their father had said to look everywhere.

So the princesses even looked in the

dark and scary Black Woods!

The princesses all called,

"Poppy, Poppy! Where are you?"

Grace was tired and worried.

She whispered a quiet prayer

for help.

Then Grace slipped and fell!

She fell in the grass by a log.

"Meow, meow," said a small voice.

Grace looked up.

She saw Poppy in the log.

Poppy was wet and messy,

but she was safe.

Grace wrapped Poppy in her cape.

The sisters rode back to the castle.

When the king saw the princesses

and Poppy, he was so happy.

The girls and Poppy were back home, safe and sound.

"Welcome home!" the king shouted.

That night, the king and

princesses ate a treat.

The king said, "We are blessed.

We have each other.

And we have five kittens,

all safe and sound."

Grace looked at Poppy.

"Thank you, God," said Princess Grace.

"But the seed falling on good soil refers to someone who hears the word and understands it."
—*Matthew 13:23*

The Princess Parables

Princess Faith's Garden Surprise

Story inspired by **Jeanna Young** & **Jacqueline Johnson**
Pictures by **Omar Aranda**

Princess Faith lived in a castle.

She had four sisters.

They are Joy, Charity, Grace, and Hope.

Their daddy is the king.

Princess Faith likes to read.

She likes flowers and

her bunny, Buttercup.

One day, Princess Faith and Buttercup

were picking flowers.

Faith walked by the castle wall.

She saw a secret door!

Princess Faith said,

"What is this door, Buttercup?

Let's find out."

Faith pushed the creaky door.

She looked into the tunnel.

There were bats and

spider webs all around.

Princess Faith walked into the tunnel.

She saw an old garden.

"This must have been a pretty garden,"

she said to Buttercup.

Then she had an idea.

Princess Faith went to see the king.

She asked daddy,

"I found a garden.

May I plant flowers in it?"

He said, "Yes. Your sisters can help."

Princess Faith told her sisters,

"Today is going to be fun.

I found a garden.

Daddy said we can plant flowers.

Come on!"

The sisters went into the tunnel.

They looked around.

Princess Charity asked,

"Are there foxes here?"

Grace asked, "Are we safe?"

Faith smiled and said yes.

Then a loud voice said,

"Why are you here?"

Princess Faith said,

"Our father, the king, said we could

plant flowers in this garden."

The guard smiled.

He said, "Very well. Have fun."

The princesses saw four plots of land in the garden.

Faith picked one.

They planted many flower seeds.

It was time to go.

But big, black birds came.

They ate up all the seeds.

"Go away!" yelled the princesses.

The next day, the princesses
planted more flower seeds.
Then they made a scarecrow.
Princess Faith said,
"Thank you! God gave me the
best sisters in the world."

The new seeds grew.

The scarecrow scared the birds away.

But the flowers died!

Faith asked the king,

"Why did my flowers die?"

He said, "That soil was not good

for planting. Try again."

Faith and her sisters planted seeds

in a new place.

The flowers grew and grew.

Faith prayed, "Thank you, God,

for the pretty flowers."

Then one night, it started to rain.

It was a big storm

with wind and thunder.

It rained for many days.

Then, one morning, it was sunny.

The princesses went to the garden.

"Oh, no," said Princess Hope.

"The flowers are gone."

"And there are weeds," said Joy.

"It is okay," Faith said.

"I think God is teaching us

a lesson about growing."

Just then, Faith saw something—

she saw one, very pretty flower.

It was in an empty part of the garden.

"The soil here must be good for plants,"
said Faith.

"This one flower grew here,
even in a big storm.
Let's plant seeds in this
part of the garden."

Weeks later, the king said to Faith,

"Your garden is beautiful!

You found the right place

for your flowers.

Your work has been rewarded."

Faith said, "Let's go see."

Faith prayed, "Thank you, God, for this garden.

Thank you for teaching me that faith can grow like seeds."

"Which of the three do you think was a neighbor to the man who fell into the hands of robbers?"
—*Luke 10:36*

The Princess Parables™

Princess Charity's Golden Heart

Story inspired by **Jeanna Young** & **Jacqueline Johnson**
Pictures by **Omar Aranda**

Princess Charity lived in a castle.

She had four sisters.

They are Joy, Faith, Grace,

and Hope.

Their daddy is the king.

Princess Charity was the

youngest princess.

She liked to run and play.

She liked adventure.

One day, Princess Charity

went to the barn.

She took care of her horse, Daisy.

Then she wanted to go for a ride.

"Where are you going today?"

asked her friend Harry.

"I will not go far, Harry," said Charity.

"I will not go to Sir Richard's land."

Princess Charity hugged Daisy's nose.

Daisy was a special gift from God.

That night the king told his
princesses many stories.
The girls loved to hear about their
daddy's trips.
Princess Charity wanted to go with
the king someday.

Charity spoke up,

"Daddy, why can't I go with you?

I want to go past the Weeping Woodlands."

The king said, "No, Charity.

That is Sir Richard's land.

You cannot go there.

Do you all understand?"

The next day, Charity packed a lunch.

She left a note to tell her sisters

she went riding.

She went to the stable to get Daisy.

Princess Charity rode to a big hill.

She looked at the kingdom.

She looked past Weeping Woodlands

to Sir Richard's land.

While Charity was eating lunch
she saw a young boy in a buggy.
He is going too fast, Charity thought.
He is too close to Sir Richard's land!

Then the buggy's wheel broke!

The boy fell out of the buggy.

Princess Charity prayed,

"How can I help that boy, God?"

Charity saw something coming.

It was a fancy coach.

"They will help the boy,"

Charity said to Daisy.

But the coach drove away.

Charity jumped on Daisy.

She rode close to the hurt boy.

Then Charity saw some of Sir

Richard's men coming.

"Thank you, Lord!" Princess Charity said.

"I know they will help."

But just like the fancy coach,

they rode away and did not help.

Princess Charity knew

she had to help the boy.

She knew he was on Sir Richard's land.

The king might get upset.

But Charity helped the boy.

She helped him get into the cart.

She took him to the castle.

The princess sisters saw Charity
and the boy in the cart.

"Who is he?" asked Faith

"Can we help too?" asked Grace.

The king asked Charity,

"Where did you find the boy?"

"Daddy, I was near Sir Richard's land.

I saw him get hurt.

I had to help!" she said.

Then they heard horses coming to

the castle.

Sir Richard was at the castle.

"Is my son here?" he asked the king.

"Yes, Princess Charity saw him get hurt.

She helped him."

Sir Richard said,

"Princess, you are a good neighbor.

You are a good friend.

I thank God for you and your kindness.

How can I show my thanks?"

Later, the king said,

"I am proud of you, Charity.

You were a good neighbor to

Sir Richard's son.

Thanks to you, our kingdoms will have

peace together again."